DATE DUE

BEAR'S ALL-NIGHT PARTY

by Bill Harley

illustrated by Melissa Ferreira

AUGUST HOUSE
Little folk

LITTLE ROCK

To Collette, from her goofy uncle—B.H.
To Tom and Pat Ferreira, who gave me life and everything else—M.F.

Published 2001 by August House LittleFolk, P.O. Box 3223, Little Rock, Arkansas 72203
501-372-5450   http://www.augusthouse.com

Book design by Mina Greenstein. Manufactured in Korea   10 9 8 7 6 5 4 3 2 1

LIBRARY OF CONGRESS CATALOGING-IN-PUBLICATION DATA
Harley, Bill, 1954–
Bear's all-night party / Bill Harley ; illustrated by Melissa Ferreira.   p.   cm.
Summary: Bear plans a party for the night of the full moon but the other animals say they will
    not come—until they are drawn to the celebration by Bear's contagious singing.
        ISBN 0-87483-572-0 (alk. paper)
        [1. Bears—Fiction. 2. Animals—Fiction. 3. Parties—Fiction. 4 Moon—Fiction]
        I. Ferreira, Melissa, 1965-ill. II.Title.   PZ7.H22655   Be 2001   00-068938

The paper used in this publication meets the minimum requirements
of the American National Standards for Information Sciences –
Permanence of Paper for Printed Library Materials,
ANSI.48-1984.

On the night of the full moon, Bear couldn't sleep. Bear didn't want to sleep. He wanted to have a party and stay up all night long with his friends. Bear said to himself, "I'm going to have a party. All my friends will come, and we'll eat, and dance, and have a good time."

The next day, Bear told his brother about his plan.

"Dumb idea," said his brother. "Ridiculous. No one is going to come. It will never work."

Bear shrugged his shaggy shoulders.

"You never know what might happen."

He planned his party and made invitations. As he delivered invitations around the neighborhood, Bear made up a song:

> *Come on out and play with me.*
> *Come on out, now, can't you see*
> *The moon will shine till the light of day?*
> *So come on out and play, come on out and play.*

Everyone told him it wouldn't work.
"No waaaaay," howled Coyote.
"No waaaay!"
Bear shrugged his shaggy shoulders.
"You never know what might happen."
He went on delivering his
invitations and singing,

Come on out and play with me.
Come on out, now, can't you see
The moon will shine till the
light of day?
So come on out and play,
come on out and play.

"Noble idea," said his best friend, Moose,
"but not very practical. I don't think
it will work, so I won't be there."

He told the birds. "Never. Forget it. No one will come," said
Blue Jay, Thrush, and Finch. "Besides, we have to get up early
to work."

Porcupine mumbled to himself, looking up from the ground,
cross-eyed and confused. "What's a party?"

"Buzz off," said the bees, grasshoppers, and crickets.

Bear shrugged his shaggy shoulders.

"You never know what might happen. I'm having a party
even if only one animal comes. And I'm an animal, and
I'm coming."

Bear prepared for his party. He swept the clearing in front of his house. He made trays of food. He practiced his song. He even took a nap.

Finally, the night of the party came. As the sun went down, Bear sat on his front steps and waited. It grew darker and darker.

No one came.
The stars came out, one by one. The moon rose
through the trees.
Still, no one came.

Finally, Bear sighed to himself, "They're all late. I guess the party will just have to start without them." He walked to the middle of the clearing, stood very straight and tall, held his front legs open wide, and said, "Let the party begin!"

He began to shuffle his feet and sing,

Come on out and play with me.
Come on out, now, can't you see
The moon will shine till the light of day?
So come on out and play, come on out and play.

As Bear sang, the moon rose through the trees, shining like an orange balloon.

Meanwhile, underground, Dad Fox was trying to put his children to bed. He had the kids cornered in their room. They were almost asleep when the ground above them started to shake.

"What's that shaking?" asked Dad Fox. "Who's singing up there?"

"We'll see!" shouted his children.

"No!" he screamed. It was too late. His kids slipped through his legs, up the steps, and out the front door. Dad Fox followed them, only to find them singing and dancing with Bear.

Come on out and play with me.
Come on out, now, can't you see . . .

"Arrgh!" Dad Fox moaned. "That Bear! No one's at his party and he's still having it!"

Just then, Wolf came through the clearing on his way to Coyote's house. "I forgot all about this party," he said. "Hello, Fox. I'm surprised to see you here."

"I'm not here," said Dad Fox, "I'm just watching." But his tail was moving back and forth in time to the music. Wolf sat down and watched too. Bear went on singing and dancing.

Just then, Moose stomped into the clearing. "EXCUSE ME!" she bellowed. "WHAT'S GOING ON HERE? WHOSE PARTY IS THIS?"

"Mine," said Bear. "Did you forget?"

"I didn't forget. I just didn't remember," said Moose. "As long as I'm here, would you like some help?"

"Sure," replied Bear. "You can sing the bass part, down low." And she did. Very low—

Bum bum bum bum bum bum bum bum

as Bear sang—

Come on out and play with me.
Come on out, now, can't you see . . .

The commotion awakened the birds. They looked down and started to talk among themselves.

"Look at everyone at Bear's party," said Blue Jay. "I guess we were wrong. We might as well join them."

The birds flew down to a branch right above Bear.

"Hey Bear," asked Finch, "do you want some help?"

"Sure," said Bear. "How about some backup singers?"

And the birds joined in—

Doo wadda badda . . . bop . . . bop
Doo wadda badda . . . bop . . . bop

with Moose singing bass—

bum bum bum bum bum bum bum bum

and Bear singing—

Come on out and play with me.
Come on out, now, can't you see . . .

More and more animals poured into the clearing to find out what they were missing. The rabbits brought a vegetable plate from a nearby garden. So many animals were dancing, there was barely room for Bear to move. He danced in one place and sang, along with Moose and the birds.

The crickets and their friends in the nearby field heard the noise coming from the forest. They hopped toward the music until they reached the party.

"This is a jumping party, Bear," said one cricket. "Can we help?"

"Sure," sang Bear. "We need some rhythm."

The bugs joined in, singing—

ka chirpa chirpa chichi
ka chirpa chirpa chichi

with the birds—

Doo wadda badda . . . bop bop
Doo wadda badda . . . bop bop

and Moose—

bum bum bum bum bum bum bum bum

and Bear—

Come on out and play with me.
Come on out, now, can't you see
The moon will shine to the light of day?
So come on out and play.

Animals were everywhere. They filled up
the clearing and hung from the branches in
the trees. Animals who had never met each other
talked for the first time. They sang and danced.

Last of all, Porcupine came into the clearing. Everybody
watched where they were stepping. Porcupine waddled
over to Bear.

"Hmmmmmmmm, ah, ah, hmmmm," Porcupine mumbled.
"How'd you get such a swinging party?"

"I don't know," said Bear. "I think it's because of the
moon."

"What's a moon?" asked Porcupine.

"What's a moon?" laughed Bear. "Up there, above
us. Everybody! Stop! Look at the moon."

Everyone stopped dancing and singing—
Porcupine, Moose, the birds, the crickets. They
all looked up at the moon.

The forest grew quiet. The full moon hung in
the sky like an enormous golden balloon,
perched in the top branches of the tallest tree.

"Hellooooo there, moon!" called Bear. "Nice night you picked to be full. Not too dark like some other nights."

The moon turned her face toward the earth. "Yes, Bear," she answered, "it's a nice night for a party."

The animals' jaws dropped open wide. They looked at Bear.

"That's impossible!" they said. "The moon has **never** spoken before."

Bear shrugged his shaggy shoulders.

"You never know what might happen."

And Moose said,

    Bum bum bum bum bum bum bum bum

and the birds joined in

    Doo wadda badda . . . bop bop
    Doo wadda badda . . . bop bop

and the crickets

> *ka chirpa chirpa chichi*
> *ka chirpa chirpa chichi*

And Bear started to sing and dance

> *Come on out and play with me.*
> *Come on out, now, can't you see*
> *The moon will shine till the light of day?*
> *So come on out and play,*
> *Come on out and play.*

ABOUT THE STORY

Bear's All-Night Party began with Bear's song. It was just me and my guitar at the kitchen table. I wrote the song one morning, trying to find a participatory story for audiences. As a storyteller, I like to find ways to remind the audience that they are part of the performance. In this story, there are three parts for audience members to sing: one part of the audience becomes the moose, one sings the part of the birds, and the last third of the audience provides the rhythm of the crickets and grasshoppers. And I'm Bear, singing his song.

For me, the relationship between song and story is intimate: songs are narrative, stories often have the rhythm and structure of song. In *Bear*, one of my favorite stories, the song drives the story forward, and many of the spoken lines function like musical refrains.

While I have written a number of children's books, I was a storyteller first. Most of my stories were told before they were written, and *Bear's All-Night Party* is no exception. Storytellers have an advantage over people who write for only the printed page. A writer, if he is lucky, has one good editor. A storyteller has dozens and dozens of audiences helping him with the story. A storyteller also has more time to let a story percolate. Every time I tell a story, something new happens. In fact, I believe I told *Bear* for three or four years before it worked well. Oddly enough, while the story grew in length, it become simpler. Different animals assumed strong personalities. My audiences showed me what was important and what worked.

Since I first told this story, it has been a lot of places. I've had a thousand people in a single audience acting like moose, birds, and crickets. It's been arranged for orchestra by my friend Paul Phillips and performed on the same program as *Peter and the Wolf*. It's been used as a sermon from the pulpit (it is, after all, about faith in the unseen). And now, best of all for me, the son of a children's writer, it appears in a book with beautiful illustrations by Melissa Ferreira. For me, what has happened with this story is a reminder of the wisdom of Bear, who hangs on to what he believes in.

You never know what might happen.

— *B.H.*

A recorded version of this story, told with original music, is available on the recording, Come On Out and Play, *available at http://www.billharley.com.*